The Duck that had NO luck

For Lara Bozas – K.P.

For Sally, Joe and Lulu – J.L.

A Red Fox Book

Published by Random House Children's Books
20 Vauxhall Bridge Road, London SW1V 2SA

A division of Random House UK Ltd
London Melbourne Sydney Auckland
Johannesburg and agencies throughout the world

Copyright © text Jonathan Long 1996
Copyright © illustrations Korky Paul 1996

1 3 5 7 9 10 8 6 4 2

First published in Great Britain by The Bodley Head Children's Books 1996

Red Fox edition 1999

Printed in Singapore

RANDOM HOUSE UK Limited Reg. No. 954009

ISBN 0 09 952961 0

The Duck that had NO luck

Jonathan Long and Korky Paul

RED FOX

There once was a duck who was down in the mouth.
He'd woken up late and missed the flight South.

'What bad luck,' said the duck. 'This isn't my day,
My friends have all flown and I don't know the way.'

So he packed up his backpack at double quick speed
With suncream and beach shorts and things he might need.

Then he spread out his wings and took off from his nest,
'I'll follow my beak,' he said, 'and hope for the best.'

But the first thing he saw was a city below
With two hundred tall towers and cars going slow.

And there on a ledge, with nowhere to play,
Perched a fat pigeon all grimy and grey.

'Hello,' said the duck. 'You look like you know.
I'm trying to fly South, which way should I go?'

'Do not fret,' said the pigeon, 'my funny-faced friend.
I'll point out the way that most birds recommend.'

But just then – guess what – the duck slipped on a tile
And fell into a drainpipe which dropped for a mile.

He rattled right down with a rat-a-tat sound
And was dumped in a dustbin back on the ground.

'What bad luck,' said the duck, looking down in the mouth.
'If this carries on, I'll never get South.'

So onwards he flew over forests and tracks,
Calling out to his friends with sad little quacks...

And there in some branches which were all of a tangle,
He spotted a parrot with his head at an angle.

...till the trees grew all jungly with dangly fronds,
And super-sized spiders and dangerous ponds.

'Hello,' said the duck. 'You look like you know.
I'm trying to fly South, which way should I go?'

'Let's see,' said the parrot, a helpful young chap.
'I'll point out the way on my extra large map.'

But just then – guess what – their tree was smashed flat
By a big-bellied man in a hard yellow hat.

The duck was sent spinning in a crazy corkscrew,
And he SPLOSHED in a swamp of yucky green goo.

'What bad luck,' said the duck, looking down in the mouth.
'If this carries on I'll never get South.'

So onwards he flew. It got hotter and hotter,
Till there was nothing but sand and no sign of water.

And there down below, flapping round on some bones,
Was a vulture whose voice had welcoming tones.

'Hello,' said the duck. 'You look like you know.
I'm trying to fly South, which way should I go?'

'My dear chap,' said the vulture, 'my poor little friend.
Just hop over here and your trouble will end.'

But just then – guess what – the vulture sprang high,
Dribbling and drooling at the thought of duck pie.

'YOW!' yelled the duck, snatching his tail from its beak
And zooming straight up in a jet-propelled streak.

There was a terrible chase at a terrible pace,
Till the duck got away – whizzing right into SPACE!

'Ooops!' said the duck, shooting past comets and stars.
'I'm sure that my friends didn't journey to Mars.'

Then he had an idea – he was very astute –
And he used his beach shorts as a pink parachute.

Down towards earth he floated and flopped.
And guess where he was when he finally stopped.

It wasn't the South – and this was a shock –
He was at the North Pole, and far from his flock.

'What bad luck,' said the duck, plonking down in the snow.
'I can't find my friends and I've nowhere to go.'

But just then he heard a loud rumbling sound
As a large group of polar bears rushed over a mound.

They were dancing about in the happiest way,
'A guest at long last,' they said. 'It's our lucky day.'

'Please stay, Mr Duck. We'll make sure you smile.
We'll throw you a party in polar bear style!'

So they sledged down the hills and whizzed round on skis.
They built snowbears and snowducks, they swam in the seas.

They threw snowballs at seagulls to hear all the squawks
And toasted fishes on fires at the end of long forks.

When he finally left, he'd been there for weeks.
He shook the bears' paws and kissed the birds' beaks.

And he made up his mind that from that day forth,
At the first sign of winter he would always fly… North.